Seven Little Hippos

By Mike Thaler
Illustrated by Jerry Smath

SIMON & SCHUSTER BOOKS FOR YOUNG READERS

Published by Simon & Schuster

New York · London · Toronto · Sydney · Tokyo · Singapore

In loving memory of Betty LaVoie
—M.T.

With love to Carrie Pace Miller
—J.S.

SIMON & SCHUSTER BOOKS FOR YOUNG READERS
Simon & Schuster Building, Rockefeller Center
1230 Avenue of the Americas, New York, New York 10020

The text of this book is set in 24 pt. Kennerly.
The illustrations are watercolor with colored pencil.
Designed by Vicki Kalajian
Manufactured in Hong Kong

10   9   8   7   6   5   4   3   2   1

Library of Congress Cataloging-in-Publication Data
Thaler, Mike, 1936-   Seven little hippos / by Mike Thaler ;
illustrated by Jerry Smath.   p.   cm.   Summary: In this variation
on the familiar counting rhyme, seven little hippos
persist in jumping on the bed, only to fall off one
by one and bump their heads.   1. Nursery rhymes.
2. Children's poetry.   [1. Nursery rhymes.   2. Hippopotamus—
Poetry.   3. Counting.]   I. Smath, Jerry, ill.   II. Title.
PZ8.3.T24Se   1991   811'.54—dc20   [E]   90-42437
ISBN 0-671-72964-0

Seven little hippos jumping on the bed.

One bounced off and bumped her head.

Momma called the doctor. The doctor said,

"No more little hippos jumping on the bed."

Six little hippos jumping on the bed.

One bounced off and bumped his head.

Momma called the doctor. The doctor said,

"No more little hippos jumping on the bed."

Five little hippos jumping on the bed.

One bounced off and bumped her head.

Momma called the doctor. The doctor said,

"No more little hippos jumping on the bed."

Four little hippos jumping on the bed.

One bounced off and bumped his head.

Momma called the doctor. The doctor said,

"No more little hippos jumping on the bed."

Three little hippos jumping on the bed.

One bounced off and bumped his head.

Momma called the doctor. The doctor said,

"No more little hippos jumping on the bed."

Two little hippos jumping on the bed.

One bounced off and bumped her head.

Momma called the doctor. The doctor said,

"No more little hippos jumping on the bed."

One little hippo jumping on the bed.

She bounced off and bumped her head.

Momma called the doctor. The doctor said,

"No more little hippos jumping on the bed."